In front of my house

To M. and L.

Originally published under the title *Devant ma maison* by Les éditions de la courte échelle inc.

Text and illustrations © 2010 Les éditions de la courte échelle inc.
English translation © 2010 Kids Can Press
English translation by Yvette Ghione

Kids Can Press acknowledges the financial support of the Government of Ontario, through the Ontario Media Development Corporation's Ontario Book Initiative; the Ontario Arts Council; the Canada Council for the Arts; and the Government of Canada, through the BPIDP, for our publishing activity.

Published in Canada by
Kids Can Press Ltd.
29 Birch Avenue
Toronto, ON M4V 1E2

Published in the U.S. by
Kids Can Press Ltd.
2250 Military Road
Tonawanda, NY 14150

www.kidscanpress.com

The artwork in this book was rendered in pencil crayon.
The text is set in Imagier.

Original edition edited by Anne-Sophie Tilly and Marie Pigeon-Labrecque
English edition edited by Yvette Ghione
Designed by Jean-François Lejeune and Sara Bourgoin

This book is smyth sewn casebound.
Manufactured in Singapore, in 5/2010 by Tien Wah Press (Pte) Ltd.

CM 10 0 9 8 7 6 5 4 3 2 1

Library and Archives Canada Cataloguing in Publication

Dubuc, Marianne, 1980–
   In front of my house / written and illustrated by Marianne Dubuc.

Translation of: Devant ma maison—
For children ages 3–7 years.
ISBN 978-1-55453-588-0

1. Space perception—Juvenile literature. 2. Vocabulary—Juvenile literature.
3. Picture books for children. I. Title.

BF469.D83 2010   j153.7'52   C2010-901540-1

Kids Can Press is a ℓorus™ Entertainment company

In front of my house

Marianne Dubuc

Kids Can Press

On a little hill,
behind a brown fence,
under a big oak tree,

is ...

my house.

In front of my house ...

a rosebush.

On the rosebush ...

a little bird.

Above the little bird ...

a window.

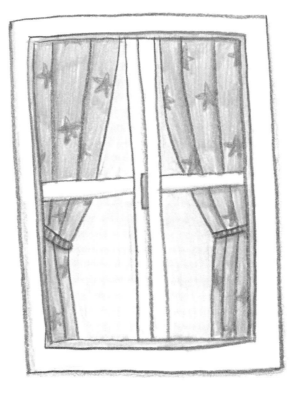

Behind the window ...

my
room.

Under my bed ...

.Whew!

Nothing at all.

Next to the nothing at all under my bed ...

an old sock.

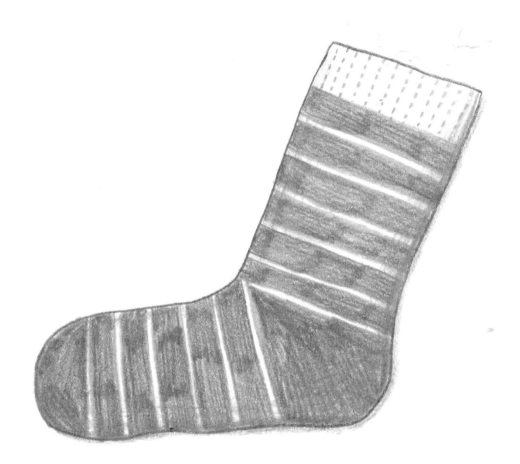

Under the old sock ...

a book of fairy tales.

In the book of fairy tales ...

a princess.

Behind the princess …

a dragon.

Behind the dragon …

a prince charming.

Under the prince charming …

a lily pad on a pond.

On the edge of the pond ...

a **bear**
fishing for breakfast.

Behind the fishing bear ...

a bush.

In the bush ...

a rabbit.

Behind the rabbit ...

a family
of rabbits.

Behind the family of rabbits ...

In the Big Bad Wolf's belly …

the Three Little Pigs,
the house made of bricks,
the house made of sticks,
the house made of straw,
one of the Seven Little Kids,
Peter,
a potful of stone soup,
Grandmother and
Little Red *Riding* Hood.

Ahead of Little Red Riding Hood …

the **hunter.**

Hooray!

Around the hunter ...

the forest.

Beyond the forest …

a moun
t
ain.

At the very top of the mountain …

a cave.

At the back of the cave …

the dark.

In the dark ...

a growl.

GRGRGRRRRR

At the other end of the growl ...

the Abominable
SNOWMAN.

Above the Abominable Snowman ...

the stars.

Next to the stars ...

a
full
moon.

Under the full moon ...

a werewolf!

Behind the werewolf …

a ghoOOOOost.

Behind the ghoooooost …

a vampire! ai yai yai.

Behind the vampire ...

the
sun!
Phew!

Around the sun ...

outer space.

In outer space …

a rocket ship.

Below the rocket ship ...

a planet.

On the planet …

Above the extraterrestrial …

a shooting star.

Under the shooting star ...

the sea.

On the sea ...

a ship.

On the ship ...

Behind the pirate ...

an enormous tentacle.

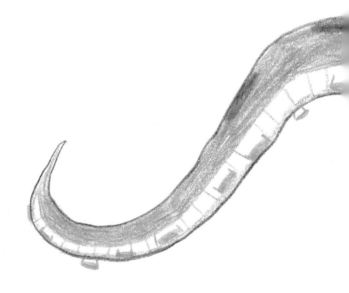

At the other end of the enormous tentacle …

a teeny-tiny octopus.

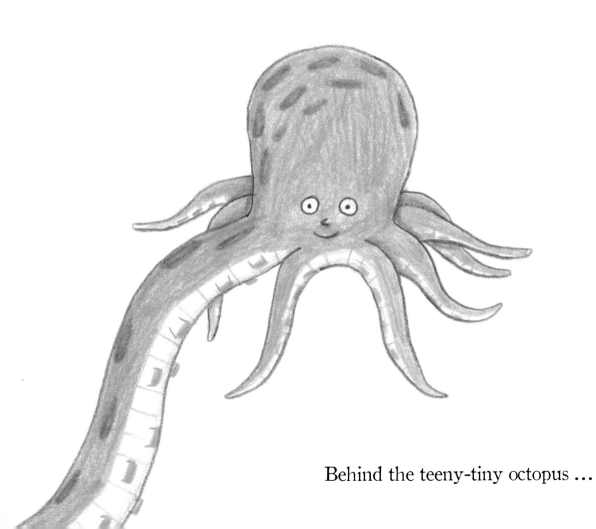

Behind the teeny-tiny octopus ...

a blue whale named Babette.

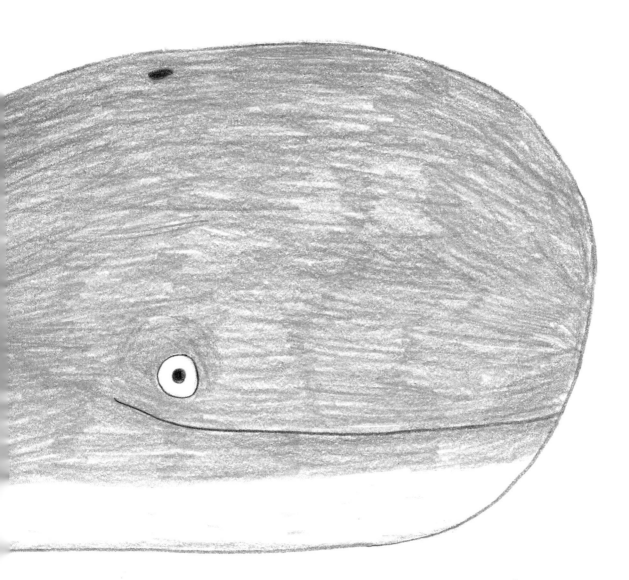

In Babette's belly …

a tuna sandwich,
an old boot,
an ocean liner,
a parrot,
an accordion,
my old teddy bear,
a little elf,
a wedge of cheese and
a magician's hat.

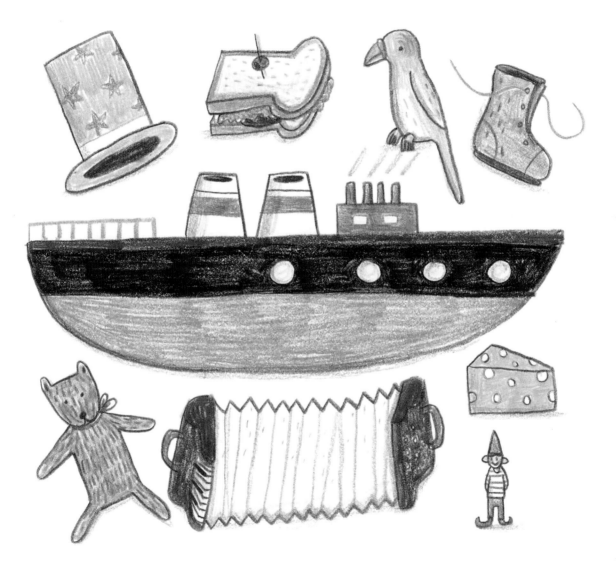

In the magician's hat …

a dove.

Above the dove …

a storm cloud.

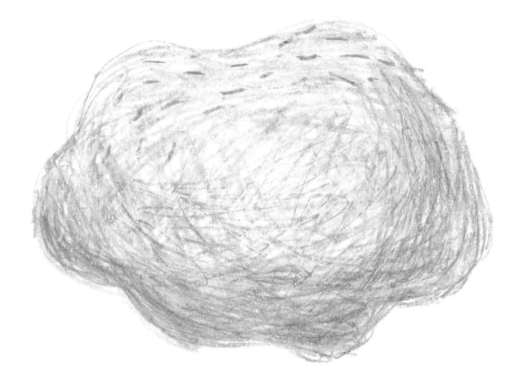

In the storm cloud …

rain.

Below the rain ...

a mama duck and her ducklings.

Behind the ducklings …

a lost baby penguin.

Not very far from the lost baby penguin …

Behind his papa …

a lion.

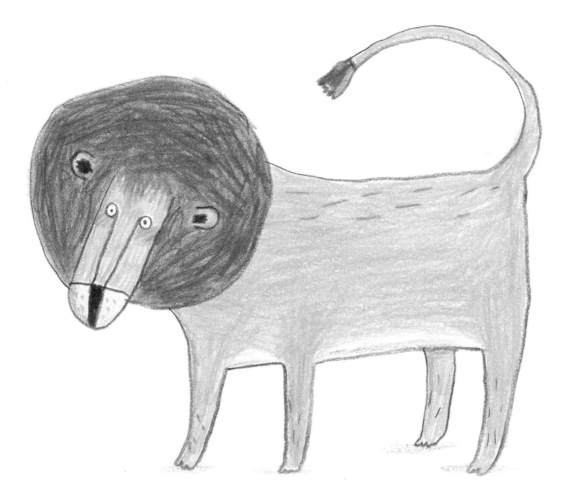

Next to the lion …

a zebra.

Next to the zebra …

a dinosaur?

Next to the dinosaur ...

an orangutan.

Around the orangutan ...

the ZOO.

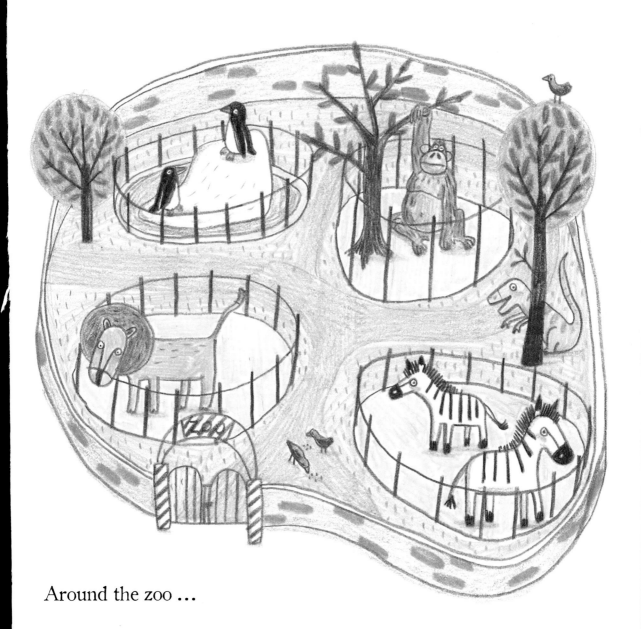

Around the zoo …

the **city.**

Beyond the city …

a little  hill.

On the little hill …

my house.